Cloud Boy

Cloud Boy

Rhode Montijo

Simon & Schuster Books for Young Readers

New York   London   Toronto   Sydney

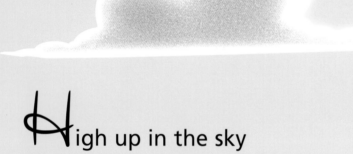

High up in the sky
lived a lonely little cloud boy.

One day a butterfly wandered high
into the clouds.

The lonely little cloud boy felt
lucky to see such a beautiful
thing, and he thought of the
greatest idea.

He gathered the fluff
from a nearby cloud and
made his own butterfly.

He sent it off for others to see.

The lonely little cloud
boy looked at the world
below and saw more
wondrous things.

He looked at the clouds above and
imagined what they could be.

He was so inspired.

He made big things.

And he made little things.

Soon the sky was filled
with his fluffy creations!

And the little cloud boy knew that
he would never be lonely again.

For Mom and Dad

SIMON & SCHUSTER BOOKS FOR YOUNG READERS
An imprint of Simon & Schuster Children's Publishing Division
1230 Avenue of the Americas, New York, New York 10020
Copyright © 2006 by Rhode Montijo
All rights reserved, including the right of reproduction in whole or in part in any form.
SIMON & SCHUSTER BOOKS FOR YOUNG READERS is a trademark of Simon & Schuster, Inc.
Book design by Daniel Roode
The text for this book is set in Frutiger.
Manufactured in China
2 4 6 8 10 9 7 5 3 1
CIP data for this book is available from the Library of Congress.
ISBN-13: 978-1-4169-0199-0
ISBN-10: 1-4169-0199-X